Boys Matter

A Boy's Book Of Self-Awareness And Self-Love For Empowerment and Compassion-Building | Motivational Book with Short Stories for Every Day | Present for Boys

John Karlsson

The book belongs to

....

....

Contents

The Snowstorm 7

Big Bully 25

A Cowboy Superhero 39

The Emergency Room 51

The Smallest Hero 69

Boy's Best Friend 87

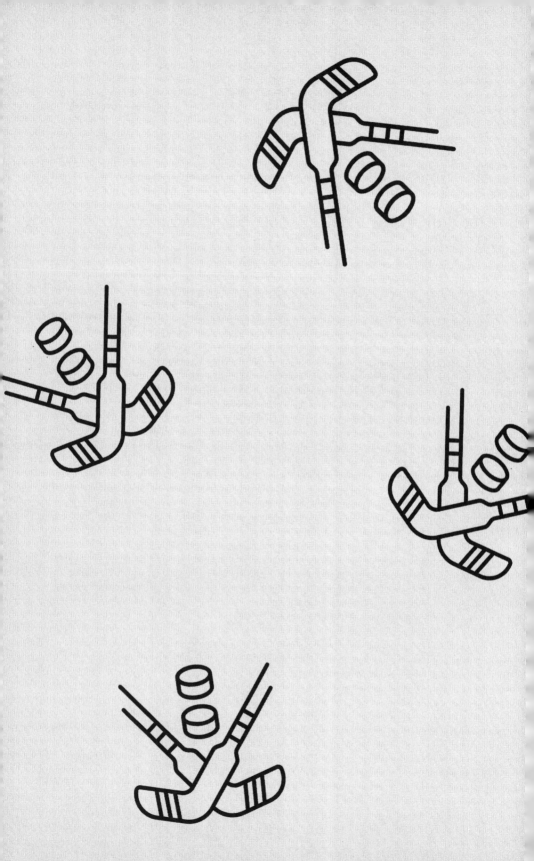

The Snowstorm

Finn was born in Alaska. He had never lived in a place that was not covered in snow for much of the year. In fact, Finn felt like he belonged in the snow. He loved everything to do with winter sports. Finn had learned to ice skate almost as soon as he learned to walk. Now, he played on the Hockey team for players ten and under.

Even though Finn was only 7, he was one of the fastest skaters. His dad had taught him how to move quickly on the ice and play hockey. Finn's dad had also played on a team as a kid.

Finn liked to help his dad around the house when it was not hockey season. Even at a young age, Finn could drive a tractor, drive the snowmobile, and help with chores like stacking wood and shoveling snow. When people from other states visited, they thought it was weird that Finn did so much at only seven, but most of the children in Alaska knew how to handle hard work. It was how things worked when you lived in what most considered the wilderness.

Finn had also been taught what to do if he encountered a bear or a moose. Both could be dangerous if you did not know how to react. He even knew how to do things like make his own snacks and take care of minor injuries. The closest town was almost an hour away. People needed to be able to handle most things on their own, even when they were very young. Finn learned most things from his dad, but his mom was the one that taught him to make the perfect sandwich and how to fry an egg so that the middle stayed runny. He had a step stool in the kitchen to make him tall enough to reach the stove safely.

In Alaska's brief summer, Finn went hunting and fishing with his dad. Anything they caught was used as food or given away to those who needed extra help. It was a tough life, but Finn was proud of all he could do. Early one morning during the beginning of the winter months, Finn was asked to go get a few pieces of wood from the shed. The wood shed was only a few hundred yards from the house, but in the biting cold, it felt like miles. Finn did not argue with his mother; he knew better. Instead, he grabbed his boots and laced them up tight. Then he grabbed his heavy, lined jacket and zipped it up all the way, tightening the hood. He grabbed a scarf before opening the door and being hit with a blast of snow and wind. The snow was light for this time of year, but in Alaska, that could change in a matter of minutes.

Finn stepped outside and let his eyes adjust to the bright sun. The reflection of the glistening snow was intense.

As Finn allowed his eyes to adjust, he took a deep breath. Even through the thick scarf, the cold filled his lungs. Finally, Finn made his way down the stairs that were covered in a fine, icy powder. With his eyes set on the shed, he walked into the wind, keeping his face down to avoid getting snow in his eyes. Ten minutes later, Finn was safe inside the shed, trying to pick which pieces of wood he would take inside.

When he was very young, Finn had learned which types of wood burned best and how each smelled when it burned. Burning pine was great for making the house smell a certain way, but oak or birch was the best option if you wanted heat. Finn could pick out each one with accuracy. He carefully looked over the large pile of wood that would last the family all winter. After choosing three decent-sized logs, Finn opened the door and was again greeted by the bright sun. He had to set the logs down to latch the door so it would not blow open in the snow.

Finn laid the logs down and turned to place the latch in place before gathering them once again. The logs were heavy on Finn's tiny frame, but he would not give up. The snowstorm had kicked up, and it was hard to see. Even though it had only been a few minutes since Finn left his house, his footprints were long gone. He could still see the house, but it was blurred by the blowing snow falling in heavy wet flakes. As Finn glanced up to ensure he was headed in the right direction, he slipped. The logs he was carrying went in different directions. Finn started to slide down a small embankment in his yard because it was so icy.

By the time Finn stopped, he was covered in snow at the bottom of a small hill. He could not see his logs, so he would have to choose new ones. Finn stood up, carefully dusting the snow off his pants and jacket. He wished he had remembered to grab his gloves before leaving the house. Once upright and dusted off, Finn looked around to get his bearings. He could see where he fell, so he knew which way he had been walking. He also knew he had to go the opposite

way to gather more logs. Finn took a deep breath, knowing that walking up the hill would not be easy. It was cold, wet, and icy already.

Finn started up the hill, half crawling with his jacket sleeves over his hands to keep them warm. Finn had to catch his breath once he finally got to the top. The wind was so cold it cut through his jacket, which was slightly wet from the fall. At the top of the hill, Finn decided the house must be to his left, so he needed to go right to get more logs. Even if he could find the logs he dropped, they would be too wet to burn now. The snow was falling in sheets, making it hard to see anything. Finn tried to decide if he should just go to the house instead of getting wood, but his mom had asked him to get some logs. He turned right to go back to the shed. Finn headed in the direction he thought was right, one slow step at a time. After a few minutes of walking, Finn looked up and around. He had no idea where he was. The snow was so heavy that he could not see his house or the shed.

"Mom!" Finn screamed into the wind. Even though he yelled as loud as he could, Finn knew that it was too noisy outside to be heard. "Mom," he yelled a little louder.

Back at the house, Finn's mom noticed he had not returned. Sometimes, Finn got sidetracked playing in the snow, but it had been almost 30 minutes since she sent him out. She glanced out the window at the blowing snow and started to worry.

"Honey," she yelled at her husband, "Finn has not come back with the logs yet."

"Give him a few more minutes. If he is not back, I will go look for him."

Finn's mom stared out the window, a knot growing in the pit of her stomach. "I don't want to wait. It is getting really bad out there," she said over her shoulder as the wind rattled the windows.

"I'm getting my boots now," Finn's father answered.

Finn's dad walked out the door into the snow-covered world that was both beautiful and scary. "Finn!" He called out as he made his way down the stairs. "Finnnnn!"

Finn started panicking when he realized he did not know where he was. His hands were cold, and he shivered as he shoved them deeper into his pockets. Finn could feel tears well up in his eyes, but he pushed them down. Crying in the cold weather could be bad news. Instead of continuing to walk, Finn stopped and tried to figure out where he was. He tried to stay calm, just like his father had taught him. Finn was used to the snow. As long as he did not panic, he would be okay. His parents probably missed him by now. Finn forced himself to look around. He recognized the tree he liked to climb in the summer. It was out past the shed. He had gone too far and missed the woodshed in the snow.

Finn knew if he turned his back to the tree, he would be looking straight at the house. So, Finn turned and determined he would just walk straight. Eventually, he would get back to his house. Finn was so cold that his fingers were hurting. He knew he had to get warm soon. Finn was also getting sleepy, but falling asleep or sitting down was dangerous when it was that cold. He forced himself to keep walking. Finn sang his favorite song as loud as he could to stay awake and keep calm.

As Finn sang, his father heard him. He could not see his son, but he could faintly hear the sound of his voice. "Finn, if you can hear me, keep talking. I'm coming." His father yelled.

Finn did not hear his father, but he kept singing as he trudged along the snowy yard. Just a few minutes had passed when Finn saw something move out of the corner of his eye. He jerked his head sideways, thinking it was a bear or wild animal. Instead, he saw his father walking straight for him. Finn ran toward his dad, happy to see a familiar face.

Finn's dad scooped him up in his arms and hugged him tight. "You okay, buddy?" He asked as Finn started to sob in his arms.

"I got lost, Dad. I'm sorry, but I'm so cold." Finn answered between tears.

"It's okay. You are all right now," Finn's dad reassured him. "Let's get you warm."

Within minutes, Finn was sitting in front of the fireplace in dry clothes with a blanket around his shoulders. His mom fixed him some hot cocoa as he explained what had happened. "I slipped and then could not see anything," Finn explained. "I did not know where I was or which direction was home. The snow was too heavy to see."

"You stayed calm and found a landmark you recognized. That was the right thing to do and was very brave. Most people would have panicked," Finn's father said with a smile. "You are pretty impressive."

Finn smiled as he sipped his hot cocoa. He let the heat cover his body and warm his icy-cold hands. He had been lucky his dad found him before frostbite set in. The rest of the day, the family shared stories of people lost in the snow. Finn was proud that he had not panicked, even though he was scared. He felt like he could handle any challenge and if he was caught in another snowstorm, he would find his way home.

Big Bully

Sean had always been small for his age. He was not too small but always at least an inch shorter than the other boys in his class. Still, Sean loved being active. His favorite sport was tee ball, and when it was not ball season, he could be found playing video games. Sean was also one of the nicest kids you could ever meet. Everyone seemed to love him. Sean was willing to help anyone if they would ask. Sadly, not all children are always kind.

At school, Sean had the same bully in kindergarten and first grade. Now, going into second grade, he was facing another year with a kid bigger than him, being a true bully. The bully's name was Randall. Randall was big for his age. He towered above the other students and used his size to his advantage. Randall would take toys and balls from other students on the playground. Randall would sometimes push smaller kids off the swings or shove them out of the way when they were trying to make a basket on the basketball court. Mostly, Randall liked to make fun of other students. Sean was a target for Randall.

Randall loved to talk about how small Sean was and call him a baby. Sometimes, he took Sean's lunch or stole a pencil when the teacher was not looking. Sean was often mad, but he never said a word. He did not understand why Randall was so mean, but Sean was taught never to be mean to others, so he wasn't. When school started, Sean hoped that Randall was not in his class. He had not seen Randall much in the summer, even though they lived on the same block.

Sean walked into his classroom on the first day and was glad to see that Randall was not in the same class. The day was quiet. When the class went outside for recess, Randall was nowhere to be seen. It seemed weird that Randall was not in school. Sean knew he had not moved away because he had seen him at the store not long ago. Sean did not think much of it as the first school days came and went.

While Sean helped his mom set the table one evening, he mentioned not seeing Randall at school. His mother stopped what she was doing and said, "I did not want to tell you because I was afraid you would be scared, but Randall is sick."

"Mom, I've been sick before. I am not afraid of a cold," Sean replied in his normal upbeat style.

"Randall is a different kind of sick. Randall has an illness that affects his kidneys. Both of his kidneys are very sick, and at least one needs to be replaced. If he does not get a new one, he will stay very sick for a long time," Sean's mother explained.

Sean listened and asked a few questions, but his mind worked quickly. He wanted to know where a new kidney could be found and how new kidneys were given. Sean's mother answered all the questions she could before they sat down for dinner. Sean was quiet during dinner, but as he helped clear the table, he announced that he wanted to help Randall.

"I did not think you got along with Randall," his mother questioned.

"He is a bully, but not just to me. Besides, everyone deserves some help when they are sick," Sean got really quiet and then asked his mom a question he was unsure he wanted an answer to. "Mom, if you give someone a kidney, do you die?"

"Oh no, honey. It is a surgery, but people can live with one kidney," she answered. "But honey, you cannot just decide to give a kidney to someone. You have to be a match, and you are so young that I am not sure I could let you donate. It would change your life."

Sean nodded to show he understood, but he still wanted to help. "Mom, how do you find out if you are a match?" Sean asked before he walked away.

"I think you have a blood test," his mother answered.

Sean thought about it for a second and headed for his room. That night,

Sean thought about ways he could help Randall. Randall may have been a bully, but maybe it was because he had been sick for a long time. Maybe Randall had been scared. Sean did not really understand why Randall was a bully, but he knew he had to help if he could.

The next day, Sean asked his mom if he could visit Randall. Sean's mom said she would call Randall's mother and ask if he was up for visitors. Two days later, Sean stood in Randall's room, staring at his bully. Randall looked pale and weak, but Sean asked if he wanted to play a game. Randall agreed, and they sat on the floor to play a video game. As they played,

Randall asked Sean what he was doing there.

"My mom told me you were sick, and I was hoping I could make you feel better," Sean explained.

Randall was quiet for a few minutes before he said, "I don't have many friends. I know I'm a bully. Thanks, I guess, for coming to visit. I get really bored when I am by myself all the time. My dad hates video games."

"I can come to visit sometime after school if you want," Sean volunteered.

"I guess that would be cool," Randall answered. Then the boys focused on hunting aliens in their video game.

"Sometimes, kids are mean because they do not know better or because they do not know how to make friends. Maybe Randall wanted friends but was going about it the wrong way," Sean's mother explained.

Sean thought about that explanation for the rest of the evening. The next morning, Sean announced that he wanted to do something to make Randall feel better. Sean wanted to help him make friends. He did not want Randall to be alone so often. Sean's mother agreed to talk to Randall's mother when Sean had a plan. By that day, after school, Sean had a plan. He had spoken to his classmates and shared that Randall was sick. Even though most people were scared to visit the class bully, a few were willing. That evening Sean's mom called Randall's mom to see if a few play dates could be set up. She agreed quickly, knowing Randall could use some friends until he could get better.

For six months, Sean and five other boys from the school visited Randall on different days. Sometimes they played board games, sometimes video games. Over time, Randall relaxed and was much nicer. Even on days when he did not feel good, he smiled when a friend came to visit. Finally, after a long wait, Randall found a match and was given a new kidney. A month later, Randall came back to school.

Sean was afraid he would start being a bully again, but Randall was nice. He played well with everyone. Sean had been brave enough to reach out to someone who was mean to him, and it changed everything. Sean no longer had a bully, but he did have a new friend.

A Cowboy Superhero

Laredo was born on a farm. He had been around animals as far back as he could remember. In fact, Laredo's mom had ridden horses until the day before she had him. There were photos all over the house of Laredo on his pony Snapjack from before he was even out of diapers. Snapjack was a little paint pony with large areas of brown and white. Snapjack was getting old, and Laredo was quickly outgrowing him. So, when Laredo's mom and dad told him it was time to move to a bigger horse, Laredo was sad but knew he could still visit Snapjack every day. Snapjack would

spend his old age out in a big field
with plenty of grass and fresh water.
He had carried dozens of children
around the field on his back.

Laredo was not afraid of the bigger horses, but Snapjack was much more than a horse; he was a friend. It was Laredo's daily job to make sure Snapjack was brushed, fed, and watered. Some nights in the summer, Laredo camped with his dad in the barn with the animals. It was fun to lay in a sleeping bag and listen to the animals get comfortable. The horses could be heard munching hay, the chickens cooed in their sleep, and the goats gathered in a stall together to fall asleep in a big pile. Laredo was a farm boy and wanted to grow up and raise horses like his parents.

Almost every weekend, Laredo and his parents went to horse shows or sales. In between, his mom and dad trained horses for other people. Sometimes, it could be scary. Laredo remembered a time when his dad had gotten thrown off a horse and limped around for a week, but it was all part of the business. Laredo was only six, but he could ride as well as most adults. He had run in his first barrel race at the age of four on Snapjack. They had not won, but running as fast as possible to try to beat the timer was fun. Laredo could not imagine how much more fun that would be on a larger horse.

The search began after announcing that Laredo would be getting a bigger horse. None of the horses on the farm were quite right, so the family started visiting barns to try out horses. The first horse that Laredo tried was a mare named Lucy. Lucy had spots all over her body that made her look like someone had dripped paint all over her. Lucy was okay, but Laredo did not feel like she was quite right. Next, he tried a tall, solid black horse named Lightning. Lightning was as fast as his name, but he was a little too fast for Laredo. Plus, Lightning was so tall that Laredo had to have help to reach his saddle. He wanted to be able to get on and off on his own at home.

Over the course of three weeks, Laredo tried out ten different horses, but none were right. He was ready to give up, but his parents said they had a few more horses for him to try out. One weekend they drove for three hours to try out all three. They were at the same barn together. First, the barn owner brought out a horse named Tank. Tank was almost as wide as he was tall. Laredo agreed to try him out, but Tank was way too fat to run, so he was a no from the beginning.

While the barn owner went to get the next horse, Laredo watched a little girl, probably the owner's daughter, play with several ponies in a field. She was brushing them and lying across their backs, just having fun. The ponies did not seem to mind the little girl climbing all over them. They were probably used to it. As Laredo watched, the next horse was brought out. This horse was a good size, not too big or small, and looked like a bigger, darker version of Snapjack.

The horse was young, but the owner said he was very calm and very fast, so Laredo had to be careful.

Laredo grabbed his helmet and climbed on Apache. Apache instantly stood at attention, like he was waiting for orders. Laredo gave him a little kick, and Apache trotted off as he had been with Laredo his whole life. The pair rode around the driveway, in the pen, and then walked into the field where the little girl was playing.

Laredo was in love; he wanted Apache to be his next horse. He wanted to take Apache home then, but he had to ask his parents. As Laredo walked Apache around the field, the little girl climbed on one of the ponies she had been playing with. Laredo watched as the pony bounced around the field, not caring that the little girl had climbed aboard. Just as Laredo was ready to go back to talk to his parents, a siren rang out near the road. It was loud and shrill. The ponies in the field spooked and took off, including the one the little girl had been riding.

Laredo watched as the little girl hung on for a few minutes but then hit the ground hard. She was lying on the ground crying. Her parents and Laredo's parents were running toward them, but so were the ponies. The little girl would be run over if Laredo did not do something. He did the only thing he could. Laredo kicked Apache hard and ran toward the little girl as fast as he could. The ponies were small, and Apache was fast. They reached the little girl before the ponies could get close. Laredo sat on Apache and blocked the ponies from the still-crying little girl.

It was only a few seconds before the girl's parents crossed the field to reach them. The little girl was scared but mostly uninjured. Her mother checked her over as the little girl calmed down. Laredo's parents were proud of their little boy, who had not been at all afraid to try to keep someone safe. He had been very brave to let Apache run as fast as he could to block the ponies. Laredo just smiled as he sat on top of Apache. He felt like a superhero or a real cowboy.

Once things calmed down, Laredo stepped down off of Apache and looked at his parents longingly. They knew he wanted the horse, but it would depend on the price. Laredo's parents asked about the price and discovered that Apache was too expensive. Laredo would have to keep looking. As they all walked back to the truck, Laredo was disappointed. Just as they were climbing in, Apache's owner called out.

"I just checked on my daughter. She has some bumps and bruises but will be fine. She called you a hero. I guess a hero should never have to leave his horse behind. Apache is yours if you promise to take great care of him," the old farmer smiled. "If you are still interested."

Laredo almost jumped out of the truck as he screamed. He would take the best care of Apache as any person could. Laredo skipped to the barn to gather his new horse and knew right away they would be friends forever.

The Emergency Room

Hunter's parents used to say that he was part monkey. Not because he was super hairy or had long arms, but because he was always climbing or jumping around. Hunter had the energy to burn and liked to use up that energy by climbing or trying flips any chance he could get. Sometimes, Hunter got in trouble at school for climbing on shelves or the closed bleachers in the gym. There was nothing he would not try to climb and very few things he would not try.

When Hunter was in kindergarten, his older brother, Logan, dared him to hold onto the ceiling fan

while it was on the highest setting.
Hunter did and was immediately
thrown to the ground. He landed with
a thud. His arm hurt for a week, but it
was just a bad bruise. Hunter's brother
also convinced him to stand on a board
teetering on a cinderblock to see if
he could be launched over the house.
Thankfully, his mother caught them
and saved Hunter from his possible
first flight. After the potential flight,
Hunter's mother made him sit down
and talk. She explained that she did not
want her children to get hurt, even if it
was on a dare. Hunter listened, but he
was sure he was too brave ever to get
hurt.

Hunter spent every day playing with his brother throughout the summer between first and second grade. His brother was three years older, and Hunter looked up to him. Logan had learned to ride a bike first and helped Hunter learn too. Logan had even

taught Hunter how to pop a wheelie
while riding. Hunter had fallen off
three times before he got it right; now,
he could pop a wheelie any time.

One hot day, Hunter's parents took
him and his brother to the local park.
Logan was learning to skateboard, and
there was a spot to practice at the park.
Hunter took his bike but liked playing
on all the playground climbing toys.
Hunter rode his bike around the paved
area of the park a few times before
parking it and going to play. Logan
was practicing his skateboarding skills
over a few small ramps as Hunter
climbed the tallest jungle gym. At
the top, Hunter stopped to watch
his brother easily roll over the small
ramps and move toward the larger

ones. He wanted to do everything his brother did; maybe he would ask for a skateboard for Christmas.

Hunter's parents were sipping cold drinks on a bench as the boys ran off some energy. Hunter climbed down and wandered over to where Logan was skating.

"Can I try?" Hunter asked as he watched his big brother in amazement.

"Uh, sure, I guess," Logan answered. Logan rolled up to Hunter to show him how to get started.

Hunter jumped straight on the board and took off. He was doing really well for the first time. Watching how well his little brother was doing made

Logan jealous. Logan knew if he just went and pushed Hunter off his skateboard, he would get in trouble, plus he loved his little brother. So, he decided to scare him instead.

"Hey, Hunter. I dare you to try the bowl," Logan called out.

The bowl was a large bowl-shaped spot for skaters and skateboarders. It went far down into the ground, and then you were supposed to be able to get all the way back up to the other side. It looked like someone had put a large concrete bowl into the ground. Since Hunter never backed down from a challenge, he was sure he could do it. Hunter carried the skateboard over to the edge and stood with one foot on it

and the other on the ground. The bowl
was huge, but Hunter refused to be
afraid.

Just as Hunter's mom looked over and yelled NO, Hunter ducked into the bowl on the skateboard. The next sound was one of Hunter screaming. He had not gotten far before he slipped off the skateboard and skidded face-first on the concrete. Hunter had not been wearing a helmet, meaning he had a deep, bleeding cut on his head. When Hunter saw the blood, he got scared and screamed. Logan was screaming, too, certain he had really hurt his brother.

Hunter's mom and dad came running. Hunter's dad scooped him up quickly, and they all ran toward the car. Hunter's mom pressed a rag to Hunter's head as they rushed to the emergency room. Hunter was so scared he was shaking. His head and arm hurt, but what scared him most was how scared everyone looked. In just a few minutes, they were rushing into the emergency room. Hunter was taken to a room almost immediately. His mother had to stand to the side as a nurse, and the doctor looked at his head.

The doctor had Hunter follow a little light inside a pen to make sure he had not been really hurt, then everyone calmed down and told Hunter to take a deep breath.

"So, tell me what happened," the doctor said as he looked at Hunter.

Hunter sniffled a few tears back before saying, "I tried to ride the bowl so I could be a skateboarder like Logan."

"Did it work?" The doctor asked with a grin.

Hunter looked down at his dirty clothes and shoes and shook his head no.

"Well, let's get you checked out," the doctor said as he looked at the cut on Hunter's head and the scrapes on his arms. "Looks like you are going to need some stitches on this head," the doctor explained.

"Stitches like on a sewing machine?" Hunter asked. He did not like the idea of his head being in a sewing machine.

"Not exactly," the doctor explained. "We will use a special medicine to numb your head, then use a special needle and thread to sew you up. It will help keep the cut closed so it can heal, and you may even have a cool scar."

The kind of stitches not on a sewing machine did not sound like much fun to Hunter, either. He tried to be brave, but as soon as the doctor left, he reached out to his mom.

"I don't want them to sew my head," Hunter admitted, holding back tears.

"I know, sweetie, but this is part of getting better. Maybe next time you won't try a new sport without a helmet.

Hunter hugged his mom closer. Being hurt was bad enough, but going to the emergency room was even scarier. There were no rooms, just curtains all around each bed. Hunter could hear people crying and yelling. Nurses and doctors ran around between rooms, most carrying medicine or shots. Sometimes, a siren would sound, and an ambulance would pull up. Hunter saw three different people wheeled in on beds. They were strapped to some kind of board so they did not get hurt even more. He was happy he had not been brought in by ambulance.

After a long wait, a doctor came back to see Hunter. The doctor explained what they were going to do. He told Hunter that it may look scary, but it would not hurt at all. He asked Hunter to be brave because it would take longer if he cried or moved around. Hunter was scared, but he wanted to be brave and then get to go home. The doctor started by rubbing some cream onto his head around the cut. It was a little sore, but the cream made his forehead numb. Then, the doctor asked him to close his eyes and tell him about his favorite sport. Hunter started talking about baseball. Hunter felt a little pinch, and then the doctor said the worst part was over. Hunter was shocked to learn he had just gotten a numbing shot so they could do the stitches.

"Okay, you are doing great, but I'm going to have to stitch you up now.

Once I'm done, you have to leave the stitches alone for ten days before we can take them out. Can you do that?" The doctor looked right at Hunter when he asked.

"I can do it. I can be tough." Hunter stated in the complete belief that he could handle anything.

"Okay. Close your eyes, but not tightly. Keep them closed until I am done. It will only take a few minutes."

Hunter closed his eyes. He could feel the doctor moving around close to him but felt no stitches. Hunter tried to think about happy things to keep his mind off of what was happening.

In just a few minutes, the doctor was done.

"Do you want to see?" The doctor asked, holding up a mirror.

Hunter shook his head yes and was amazed to find out he had five tiny stitches on one side of his forehead, right above his eyebrow. Hunter liked the way the stitches made him look tough.

"You are one brave little dude," the doctor said as he told Hunter he could leave. "But no more skateboarding without a helmet."

"Agreed!" Hunter said as he climbed off the bed and headed for the door.

Logan was waiting with Hunter's dad in the waiting room. Logan was impressed at how brave his brother had been through everything. "I promise I will teach you the right way to ride soon," Logan said as they headed toward the car. Hunter may not have been great at skateboarding yet, but he was the bravest six-year-old that Logan had ever met.

The Smallest Hero

Andre lived in a small village many, many years ago. He lived during a time when things were new and magical. People were just learning about using fire to cook and building houses made of a mud and straw mixture. The biggest threat to Andre's village was the dragons living in the mountains high above the clouds. Normally, the dragons and villagers lived peacefully. But if someone angered the dragons, they could stomp through the village, breathing fire and causing damage.

Even though Andre was only five, he knew about the dragons. Everyone knew about the fire-breathing beasts that lived among the clouds. Sometimes, in the early morning, the dragons could be seen flying in the sky. Andre loved to sneak out of his house, watching them dip and dive in the sky. Some dragons were smaller than the others, but they were still huge. The dragons had beautiful scales along their backs that glittered in the morning sun. Andre's favorite had unique red, blue, and green patches. When Andre got to see the dragons out flying, he imagined they were playing a game. They flew all around, their giant wings open and filling the horizon. It was impressive as long as the dragons stayed in the air.

In the late autumn, the dragons would not come out as often. They retreated to the caves to care for their eggs. Even though dragons grew very large, they came from very small eggs. Once hatched, they grew quickly and could fly when only a few days old. Still, the mother dragons would protect their eggs from anyone and everything for the few weeks it took to hatch. Sometimes, people would try to steal the eggs so they could have pet dragons, but the mothers would come after the thief and do whatever she could to take her egg back home. An angry mother dragon was a terrifying thing to face.

However, when the baby dragons were born, they were very cute. They were so tiny and had silvery scales along their backs. The color did not come in for the first few weeks. They grew quickly, doubling in size almost daily. Within a few days, the baby dragons could be seen practicing flapping their wings and taking short flights. Baby dragons were not as dangerous as the adults. They could get big, but it took a few months before they could control their flight or use fire breathing. Andre had always wanted to get close to the dragons, but he also knew how dangerous they could be. Even when Andre was little, he had been told the stories of dragons being dangerous to villagers. Parents told all the children to keep them away from the high caves where the dragons lived. Still, Andre was fascinated by the creatures that ruled the sky.

One early morning, Andre saw the dragons acting strange. They usually played in the sky, but now they were panicking, swooping down toward one spot repeatedly. It was like something important was in that spot, but the dragons could not get where they wanted. Andre watched a few dragons try to go low into the rocks, but all were stopped short of whatever was in the area. Andre sat outside watching the dragons for hours. A crowd of people had gathered to watch them as well. It was odd for the dragons to stay out during the daytime. They preferred early mornings and evenings to fly and play. The dragons were out all day, making the same swooping motion in the same spot.

That night, fearing what the dragons may do if they became more upset, a group of villagers hiked to the spot the dragons seemed focused on. As they hiked, the villagers could hear a wild animal crying, almost howling, as if in pain. The villagers moved very slowly as they got near the spot. A large female dragon with shimmering blue scales stood guard. She was the one making the horrible noise. The villagers moved purposefully and in complete silence to see what the dragon was guarding. That is when they saw something amazing. A single, small dragon egg had fallen and rolled between two large stones with pointed tops. The dragons were too large to get into the small space. Sadly, the villagers were also too big. The space was tiny, not much bigger than a child.

Knowing why the dragons acted odd, the villagers returned to the village. Word spread quickly about what was happening. The villagers wanted to help the dragon to retrieve her egg so they could stay safe, but no one could figure out how to get to the lone egg in such a small space. Andre tried to tell his father and others that he could fit. He was very small, but no one would listen because he was a child. All day, Andre tried to explain that he knew he could fit. He often hid in small spaces when he was playing. Still, no one would listen.

Late that night, Andre decided he was going to help. He set out in the darkness to the spot where the dragon was waiting, guarding her egg. The pathway was scary. There were long, jagged rocks on either side. The moon was not out, and the shadows looked like monsters as Andre made his way up the winding path. Even though Andre was tired, he kept going. He had a plan. Andre made his way up the path for hours to just the right spot. As he got closer, he could hear the dragon breathing and crying. Andre could see the huge scales he had always wanted to touch, but he knew it was not safe. The dragon was even larger than he had imagined.

Very slowly, Andre inched past the sleeping dragon. He found the small hole where the egg was nestled deep inside. It was dark and cold as Andre leaned down to get a better look. The shiny, silvery egg was at the back, just waiting to be rescued. Just as Andre stepped back, he felt the breath of the mother dragon on his back. He turned slowly to face one large eye staring him down. The dragon looked closely at Andre. Andre thought he was about to be eaten, but the dragon seemed to understand what was happening. Instead of eating Andre, she nudged him forward toward the spot where the egg rested. Andre understood.

Andre nodded to the dragon, not knowing if it would understand if he spoke. Andre lifted his hands and knees and started crawling into the dark crevice. He could feel the rocks and dirt digging into his skin as he slowly walked deeper toward the shimmering egg. Andre could not see anything. The small amount of moonlight that snuck through did little to light the way. Andre felt spiderwebs touch his face and hoped no creatures lived in the dark little corner. Finally, Andre reached the egg. Though it was small in comparison to the dragon, the egg was almost the same size as Andre.

Andre managed to get behind the egg and gently started rolling it toward the entrance. The movement was hard. Andres was on his knees on the cold, rocky ground and trying to push while also moving forward. The whole time he could see the eye of the mother dragon, who basically had him trapped as he tried to return her egg. Andre worked for what felt like hours. He was cold, hungry, and hurting from the crawling and pushing. Finally, he could see the entrance. The mother dragon took a single step back, allowing the egg to be pushed out. As soon as the egg was free, the dragon grabbed it gently in her mouth and flew high up to her cave.

Andre made his way out too. He was impressed with himself for helping a dragon all alone, but he was also exhausted. He still had to walk back to the village, and no one would believe he had been that close to a dragon and survived. Still, Andre had been brave and helpful, so it did not matter if anyone ever knew. Andre stood up, stretching his arms and legs. He wanted to nap but knew he should get home. Plus, being out on the cliffs at night with all the wild creatures was probably not safe. As Andre slowly returned to his home, he could see the sun rising. His parents would be mad if he were not at home and in bed, but he could not move any faster.

As the sun started to peak over the horizon, he heard the dragons flying overhead. Normally, Andre would stop and watch them, but he did not have time. Suddenly, a dragon flew very close. Andre recognized it as the mother dragon who had been so happy to get her egg back. Andre pressed himself close to the rocks as she flew closer and closer. He was scared, just like he had been taught to be. Then, the dragon did something amazing. She hovered right beside Andre, looking at him. Andre could not stop himself; he reached out to touch her nose. Andre could feel her hot breath on his hand as he petted the magnificent beast. He was so excited; he forgot how dangerous this could be. Andre could not help himself; he leaned in and kissed the dragon on the nose. He did not fear her, knowing she was just a mother who wanted to keep her baby safe.

The dragon stayed with Andre, ensuring he was safe as he walked. Even when Andre got to his village, the dragon stayed nearby. As the villagers began to wake up and leave their homes, they were shocked to see a dragon quietly flying beside a little boy. As Andre got close enough to be recognized, the townspeople ran toward him. They thought he was in danger. Andre told everyone what happened and how the dragon had kept him safe. He showed them that the dragons were just protecting their own, just like the people in the village did. The dragon landed on the ground as Andre showed everyone how to pet her nose carefully.

That day changed everything. Andre had been brave and taught the villagers something special. No one ever tried to steal dragon eggs again. In fact, the dragons never attacked again. The villagers were protected, and the dragons could also live their lives. Sometimes, the mother dragons would bring their babies down to visit the villagers. Everyone took turns petting the shimmering scales on the babies and mothers. It was an amazing thing to be part of, and it happened all because one little boy decided to be a hero and show kindness.

Boy's Best Friend

Michael was a happy kid, but he was pretty lonely. He was six years old, and even though he loved not having any brothers or sisters, it would have been nice to have someone to play with. When Michael was in school, he talked to a few other children in his class, but he did not have a best friend. Michael was pretty sure it was because he could not run and play like the other kids.

When Michael was born, he was very sick. When he got sick, the illness damaged one of his legs. Now Michael had to walk with a crutch. The crutch was not so bad. It was better than when Michael had to use a walker. The kids in his neighborhood used to tell him he looked like a little old man. At least now, Michael could move faster and build up his strength. His doctor told him he would get stronger and learn to run with practice. Still, Michael wanted to be like the other boys and ride bikes or play soccer. It just was not possible for him yet.

Sometimes, Michael would have a friend over to play video games or go swimming. He was good at both those things, but not many friends wanted to be stuck doing only those two things. This meant Michael spent most of his time with adults. Michael's parents loved him and would ensure he always had fun toys, but he wanted a friend.

One warm summer afternoon, Michael and his dad were out walking. Michael's muscles needed lots of walking to get strong. As Michael and his dad walked down a tree-lined dirt road, something small in the grass caught Michael's eye.

"Dad, there is something in the grass," Michael said, walking toward the moving creature.

"Whatever it is, do not touch it until I can make sure it is safe," his dad called back.

Michael stood over the tiny creature, watching it wriggle in the tall grass. When his dad reached the same spot, they both knelt down to get a closer look. Michael's dad reached down to pick up the creature, barely bigger than a quarter. He examined it closely before announcing that it was a baby squirrel that must have fallen from the nest. Michael and his dad looked all around to find the nest but found no squirrel nests.

"Maybe it was blown out of a nest somewhere. We have had lots of storms lately," Michael's dad wondered aloud.

"Dad, we can't leave it here. Something will eat it, or it will freeze.

Can we take it home?" Michael begged with his eyes.

"I don't know if we can take care of a baby squirrel," Michael's dad thought about what to do, "We can take it home, and I will call the wildlife specialist to see what to do."

Carefully, Michael's dad placed the tiny creature in Michael's hand, and they walked back toward their home. At home, Michael filled a shoebox with some fuzzy blanket squares and gave the tiny creature a cup full of water to drink. The squirrel curled up and seemed to fall asleep while Michael watched. As Michael watched over the sleeping creature, his dad called the wildlife rescue center that was just a few miles from their home.

"Hello, is this wildlife rescue? We found a baby squirrel and could not find a nest. Can we bring it to you?" Michael could hear his dad speaking on the phone, but he hoped that they could keep the squirrel.

When Michael's dad returned to the room, he explained that they needed to take the squirrel in immediately. It was so young that it needed special care. Michael was sad, but he understood the importance of giving the baby the best care. They loaded into the car, with Michael carrying the tiny baby in the shoebox. Within minutes, they pulled into the wildlife rescue.

Michael carefully carried the shoebox with one hand as he used his crutch with the other. A very nice lady met them at the door.

"Are you the ones that found the squirrel?" She asked, looking into the box.

Michael spoke up, "Yeah. Will it be okay?"

The lady picked up the tiny little bundle and examined it. "Well, it is very young and needs lots of care, but we will do our best. You are welcome to call or visit anytime to check on him. Would you like to name him since you are the rescuer?"

Michael thought about the perfect name. He considered Thor and Roger, even Flower, but then he thought about what he wanted most in the world and chose the name Buddy. Buddy was taken to a special room and put in an incubator to keep him warm. He was given a tiny stuffed bunny to curl up with and a big fluffy blanket to dig in if he got cold. The kind lady explained that Buddy would need to be given food through a tiny bottle every few hours, but if he ate well, he should be fine. Buddy would be released into the wild to be like other squirrels when he grew up and got strong. Michael was happy for Buddy but sad to leave him behind. On the way home, Michael asked his dad if they could visit in a few days. His dad agreed.

That night, Michael dreamed about Buddy. He thought about how lucky squirrels were to be able to jump and climb. Michael wished he could run and climb like a squirrel, and maybe then he would have more friends. The next morning Michael woke up sad because he missed Buddy. After some begging, Michael convinced his dad to call and check on Buddy. Michael's dad called the rescue, and the kind lady from the day before said Buddy had done well. He was eating from a bottle, but he was still very weak. Michael felt better, but he could not get Buddy off his mind. Buddy would be the coolest pet ever, even if he were not really a pet. Michael wondered if Buddy remembered him.

On Saturday, four days after Buddy had been found, Michael and his dad visited him at the rescue. Michael was allowed to help with Buddy's feeding if he was careful and did just what he was told. Watching the little bald, squirmy baby squirrel drink from a tiny bottle was exciting. When Buddy was finished eating, Michael carefully placed him back in his warm bed and watched as he scooted around to get comfortable. Buddy's eyes were just starting to open and looked like sparkling black dots on his pink body.

Over the next few weeks, Michael visited Buddy often. He watched as he started growing fur and trying to play in his little enclosure. About three weeks after Buddy had been taken to the rescue, Michael asked why he was not climbing and playing yet. The nice lady explained that Buddy had been injured when he fell or got blown out of the nest. Buddy had an injured foot that was not healing. It was probably permanently damaged. Michael looked at his own crutch propped against the chair.

"I know how he feels. How is he going to play with the other squirrels?" Michael asked.

"Buddy will not ever be able to climb and play like the others," the lady explained, "we will have to keep him here or find him a home that can take care of him."

Michael's eyes lit up. "Can he come to live with me?"

"If your parents agree, I see no reason why you could not be Buddy's owner. He will be lots of work. Are you sure you can handle a squirrel that cannot walk correctly?" The lady asked.

"I can do it! I understand how he feels. I bet he can learn to climb in his own time. We can practice together," Michael was so excited to ask his dad if Buddy could live with them.

Michael's dad was not sure about having a squirrel as a pet. He asked the rescue lady what they would need as far as food, a cage, toys, and anything extra. She explained everything and even wrote out a list. Michael's dad agreed that Michael could keep Buddy as a pet if he did all the work. Michael was so happy that he could not quit smiling. Michael had to say goodbye to Buddy one last time so they could go get all the supplies they needed. Buddy would be old enough to leave and eat on his own in two weeks, so Michael had that much time to get ready.

At the pet store, Michael picked out a giant cage with a hammock for Buddy to rest in. It had little climbing ladders, so he could practice as much as he wanted. Michael also picked out food, treats, and a few toys for Buddy to chew on. Lastly, he picked out a nice warm blanket to keep Buddy warm when it was time to sleep. Once all that stuff was at home, Michael helped his dad set it up in his room. They found a big branch outside to put in the cage to help Buddy practice climbing in case he ever wanted to try climbing outside.

It seemed like the two weeks to bring Buddy home took forever. Even though Michael visited a few times, the days seemed long. When it was finally time to go get Buddy to bring him home, Michael almost ran to the car. He had a small carrier to bring Buddy to his forever home. At the rescue, the lady who had been caring for Buddy brought him out to put him in the carrier. She gave him the small stuffed bunny that had been with him since the first night and asked Michael to call her if he needed any help. Michael agreed as he stared at Buddy through the mesh of the carrier.

At home, Michael carefully placed Buddy in his new cage in the hammock. Buddy had gotten much bigger. He had a short furry tail that twitched all the time and more than doubled in size. Buddy walked a little wobbly because of the damaged foot, but Michael did not mind. He already loved Buddy. That night, Michael held Buddy, petting his soft fur. When Buddy started to fall asleep, Michael carefully put him in his cage, checking to make sure he had food and water. Michael then went to bed and watched as his new pet slept quietly. When Michael fell asleep, he dreamed of all the adventures that he and Buddy would have.

The rest of the summer went by quickly. Michael took Buddy out for walks every day. At first, Buddy rode in Michael's shirt pocket, but soon he was riding on Michael's shoulder. People were always surprised to see a squirrel as a pet, but Michael loved him. Michael and Buddy played every day. Buddy learned his name and would come when called. He was even starting to learn to climb. Michael knew how hard it was to learn to use a hurt leg, so he encouraged Buddy, giving him lots of pets each time he climbed something. By the end of summer, Buddy was running all around the house. He could climb up the chair and sofa in seconds. Buddy was even learning to jump from the sofa to the shelf. Michael loved watching his new best friend having fun. When it was warm in the afternoons, Buddy and Michael would go outside to play. Buddy liked to run around on the grass and even tried to climb up a few trees, even if he did not get very far. Michael would run around trying to keep up with Buddy. He could run pretty fast by the time school started back.

Michael did not want to leave Buddy when the school year started, but his dad promised Buddy would be okay. Michael ensured his food and water bowl were full before leaving

for school. "I'll miss you, Buddy," Michael said as he got dressed, "you are my best friend."

Buddy chattered back to Michael as if they were actually talking. Michael smiled. He thought back to that moment he saw Buddy in the grass and when he first had to leave him at the rescue. Most people would not want a squirrel with a messed-up foot, but Michael thought it made Buddy special. Michael's dad told him that he was Buddy's hero, but Michael felt like Buddy had saved him. That one act of kindness had changed Michael's life for the better.

Disclaimer

This book contains opinions and ideas of the author and is meant to teach the reader informative and helpful knowledge while due care should be taken by the user in the application of the information provided. The instructions and strategies are possibly not right for every reader and there is no guarantee that they work for everyone. Using this book and implementing the information/recipes therein contained is explicitly your own responsibility and risk. This work with all its contents, does not guarantee correctness, completion, quality or correctness of the provided information. Misinformation or misprints cannot be completely eliminated.

Made in the USA
Las Vegas, NV
09 August 2023

75866819R00065